BEAR
MOVES

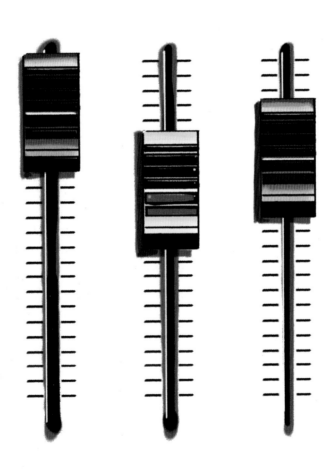

First published 2019 by Walker Entertainment,
an imprint of Walker Books Ltd
87 Vauxhall Walk, London SE11 5HJ

2 4 6 8 10 9 7 5 3 1

Text © 2018 Ben Bailey Smith • Illustrations © 2018 Sav Akyüz

The right of Ben Bailey Smith and Sav Akyüz to be identified as author
and illustrator respectively of this work has been asserted by them in
accordance with the Copyright, Designs and Patents Act 1988.

This book has been typeset in Bokka Solid. • Printed in Malaysia

British Library Cataloguing in Publication Data:
a catalogue record for this book is available from the British Library

ISBN 978-1-4063-5926-8

www.walker.co.uk

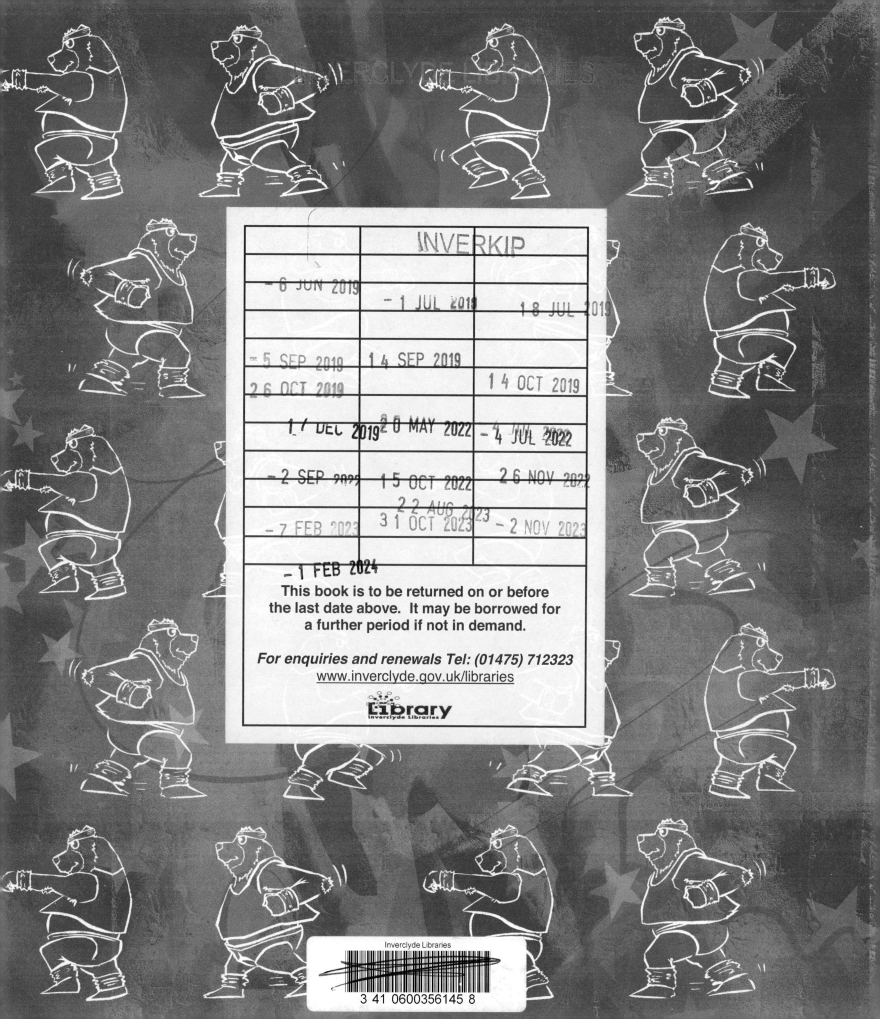

BEAR MOVES

SIDE A:

For my Godsons,
Felix and Laurie
B.B.S.

SIDE B:

For Mum,
love always x
S.A.

Ben Bailey Smith
aka "Doc Brown"
and
Sav Akyüz

WALKER
ENTERTAINMENT

Knock! Knock! Who's there? Munch. munch. My lunch. I do magic. Most bears won't. Now you see me... Now you don't! Look behind you. Boo! Do you like games? I do, too. Cops and robbers! That's my favourite. Doughnut's missing! Guess who ate it? Fun with friends, that's the main thing. Favourite hobby? Probably painting. I am Bear, and I was there... Now I'm gone... So long! I am Bear. And I am bare. The suit I wear has purple hair. In my tummy? Mostly honey. Here's a thingy I find funny...

I am Bear.

But I'm not bare.
And this is not my underwear.

These are just the clothes I choose
When I'm in a dancing mood.

Here's a move called Furry Breaking

Put your paws up!
Get 'em shaking.

Get up, get down,
hit the ground...

On your back start spinning round.

Hold a stance that goes like this!

OK, Bunny!
Music switch!

This one's called the Running Bear.
(You run but don't go anywhere.)

Bears think they're like me?
They're so not!
What bears you know
do the Robot?

Get down like me? I don't think so.
How low can you go in limbo?

One for mums and dads
and whatnot?
Grab a friend and do
the Foxtrot!

Move your bodies nice and smooth.

Here's a treat for kids and grown-ups...
All you need's a box of doughnuts!

Eat these and you've every chance
of doing a great Belly Dance!

Giant doughnuts would be cooler...
Climb inside and do the Hula!

No more doughnuts in the pack,
time to have a different snack.

We can do the
Twist this time,
Turn around and
Wind behinds!

One more dance and this sounds crazy
But I need the perfect lady.

Someone who is just my size
With paws that hit the floor and glide.

Someone sweeter than a mango.

Perfect!
It takes two to Tango!

Careful though, how low you stoop,
Dancing can be tough...

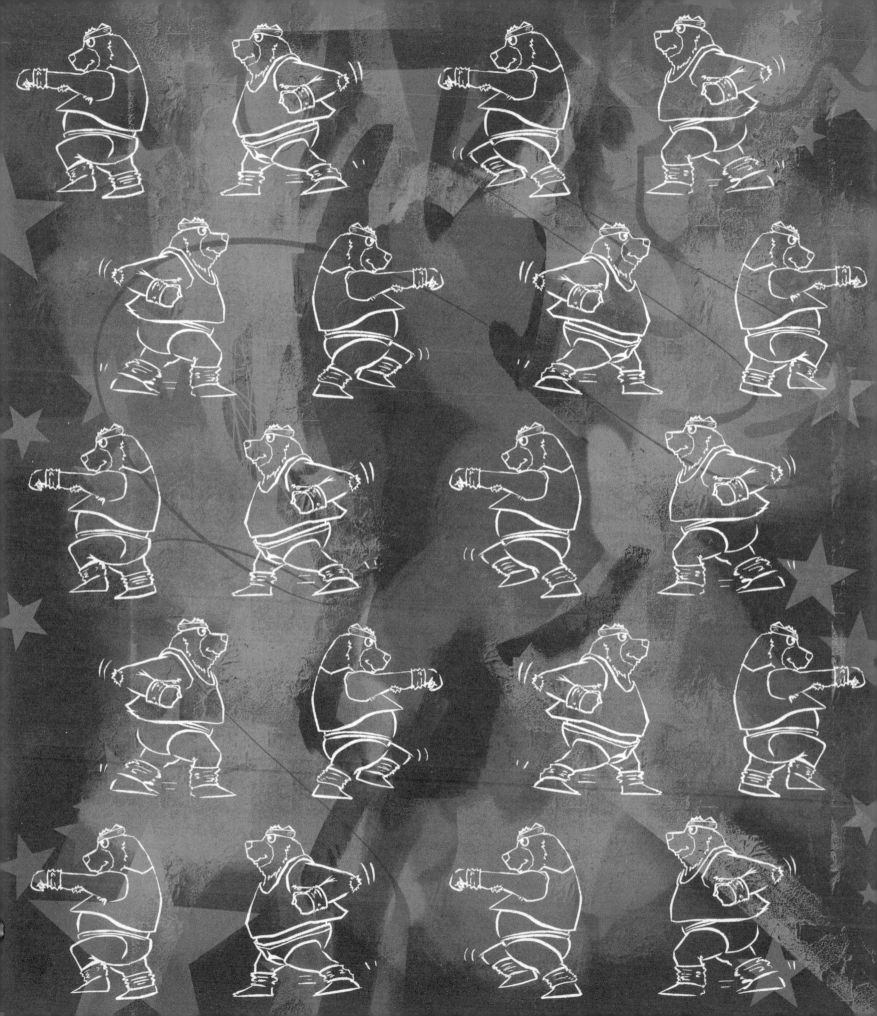